OLIVIA™
and Her Ducklings

adapted by Veera Hiranandani
based on the screenplay written by Eryk Casemiro and Kate Boutiler
illustrated by Shane L. Johnson

Ready-to-Read

Simon Spotlight
New York London Toronto Sydney

Olivia is painting a picture
of Ian.
But Ian will not stand still.
He has an itchy nose.

Olivia looks for something else to paint.
She sees some ducks.
Maybe she can paint a picture of them.

"Poor little ducks,"

says Olivia.

"They want their mother."

The ducks cannot climb
the hill.
Olivia and Ian help them.

"Come on, ducks!" says Olivia.

"Quack!" says Ian.

They did it!

Olivia wants to stay

with the ducks.

But it is time to go home.

"Good-bye, ducks!"

says Olivia.

At home, Olivia paints
a picture of flowers.
She paints her flowers
red, yellow, and pink.

Quack!

"Very funny, Ian. Please stop," says Olivia.

"Stop what?" asks Ian.

“Look!” says Olivia.

“The ducks followed us home!”

"I guess they really, really like me!" Olivia says.

"Quack!" say the ducks.

Olivia's mom sees the ducks.

"Can we keep them?"

asks Olivia.

“I’m sorry, Olivia.
The pond is their home,”
says her mom.

“The ducks have to
go back in the morning,”
her mom says.

At least the ducks can stay
for a little while.
"Who wants to play
hide-and-seek?"
Olivia asks.

"I do!" says Ian.
"Do not look behind
the piano!"
Olivia shuts her eyes.
She counts to three.

Olivia looks in the kitchen.

She does not see any ducks.

Olivia looks in the
living room.
But she does not see
any ducks.

Olivia cannot find
the ducks.
"Ian! Please help
me!" calls Olivia.

“Olivia! I know where
the ducks are!
Come to the bathroom!”
says Ian.

The ducks are in the bathtub!

"Just because I hate baths

does not mean ducks

hate them too," says Ian.

After their swim,
it is time for bed.
"Would you like me
to read you a book?"
Olivia asks the ducks.

But the ducks are asleep.

“Good night, ducks,” says Olivia.

Soon Olivia will be asleep too.

“You did a wonderful job
with your garden,”
says Father at bedtime.
“I do not think we will have
any more flies,” says Olivia.
“Good night, Olivia!”

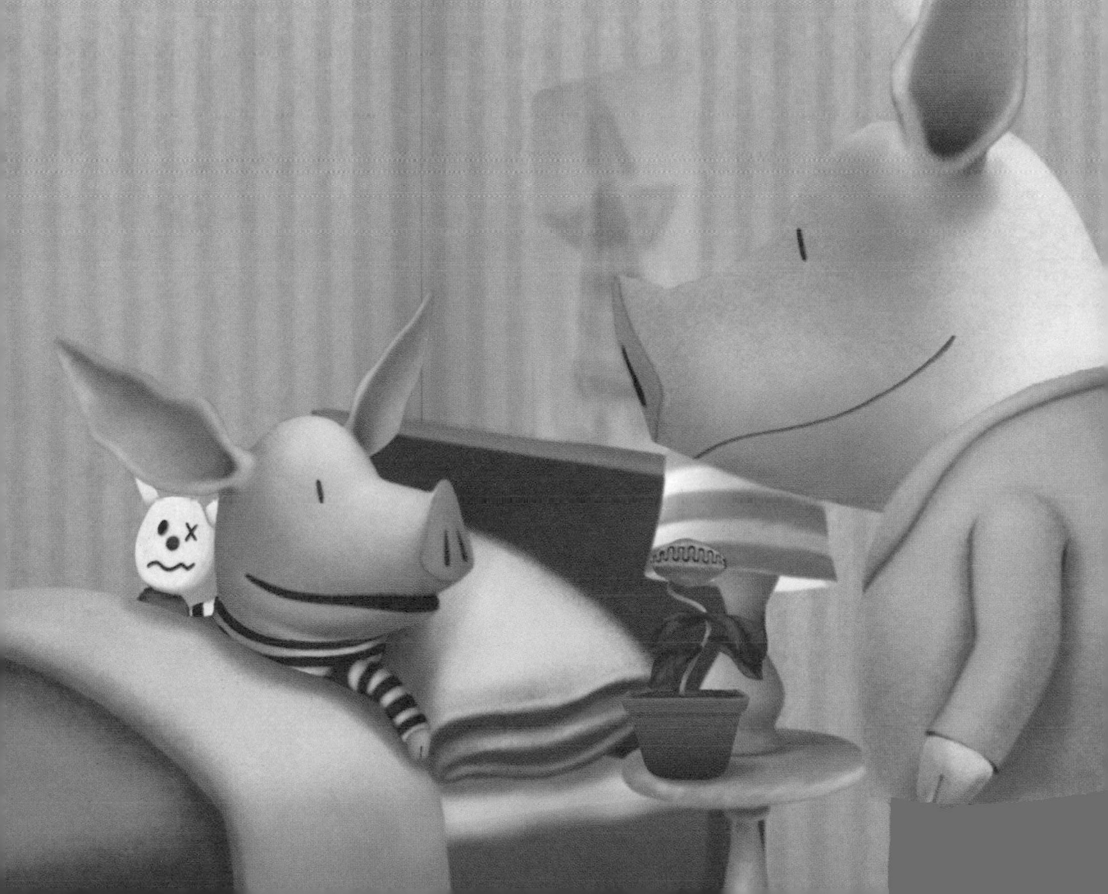

"That is a Venus flytrap,"
says Mrs. Hoggenmuller.
"I will call it a surprise plant,"
says Olivia.
"That fly sure looked
surprised!"

All of the children bring
their plants to school.
"This is my surprise plant!"
says Olivia.
Snap!
Olivia's plant closes around
a fly.

Back at her house,
Olivia checks on her plants.
“My surprise seeds have
grown into surprise plants!”

a dinosaur bone,"
says Mrs. Hoggenmuller.
"I think it is a dog toy.
Look! It is attracting flies."

“I found a dinosaur bone
in my garden,”
says Olivia at school.
“I do not think that is

“I am not sure,” says Julian.

“Look!” says Olivia.
She holds up a bone.
“I think it is a
dinosaur bone.”

"Oh, Perry!" says Olivia.
"I will just have to
plant more seeds.
And I will have to be even
more patient."

Oh no!

Perry is digging a hole right where Olivia planted her seeds.

Olivia tells her plants
lots of stories.
She shows her plants
how she rides a scooter.
She sings songs to her
plants.

"Hello, plants," says Olivia.
"I hope that you grow
so I will know what you are."

“I can do that!” says Olivia.

"Did you know that talking to plants can help them grow faster?" asks Father.

"This is going to be the best
surprise garden ever,"
she tells Julian.

At home Olivia digs in
her yard.
Perry helps her dig.

“These are surprise seeds.”

"What kind of seeds
are these?" asks Olivia.
"I do not know,"
says Mrs. Hoggenmuller.

"What will we grow?"
asks Olivia.
"Sprouts, herbs, flowers,
and beans,"
says Mrs. Hoggenmuller.
"Come choose your seeds!"

"Each student will get
a packet of seeds.
You will plant
the seeds at home."

"It is springtime, children!"
says Mrs. Hoggenmuller.
"We will plant our own gardens.

Based on the TV series *OLIVIA*™ as seen on Nickelodeon™

SIMON SPOTLIGHT
An imprint of Simon & Schuster Children's Publishing Division
1230 Avenue of the Americas, New York, New York 10020

For information about special discounts for bulk purchases, please contact Simon & Schuster
Special Sales at 1-866-506-1949 or business@simonandschuster.com.
Manufactured in the United States of America 2012 LAK
This Simon Spotlight edition 2011
2 3 4 5 6 7 8 9 10
ISBN 978-1-4424-5289-3
These titles were originally published individually by Simon Spotlight.

OLIVIA™
Plants a Garden

adapted by Emily Sollinger
based on the screenplay written by Rachel Ruderman
and Laurie Israel
illustrated by Jared Osterhold

Ready-to-Read

Simon Spotlight
New York London Toronto Sydney